JACOB'S VALENTINE

Written and illustrated by JoAnne DeKeuster

ISBN: **0-9975162-0-8**
ISBN 13: **978-0-9975162-0-3**
Library of Congress Control Number: **2016939513**
LCCN Imprint Name: Enchanted Circle Pottery, Taos, NM

To all children grieving the loss of a loved one

Acknowledgements

A special thanks to my mother, Irene Dittrich, the woman who always encouraged her little girl to draw.

Many thanks to my husband, Kevin, for all his support through the trials and tribulations of writing and illustrating my first book.

Jacob woke up and jumped out of bed. As he stretched and yawned, his body shook with excitement.

"Yes! Today is Valentine's Day!"

For weeks Jacob had been counting down the days, waiting for this special day. For the past two years, Valentine's Day had been a terribly sad day for him because he had been unable to give his mother a valentine. Valentine's Day had been one of his mother's favorite days.

This year was different. Jacob was determined to give his mother a valentine. He had a plan, and he was sure his plan would work.

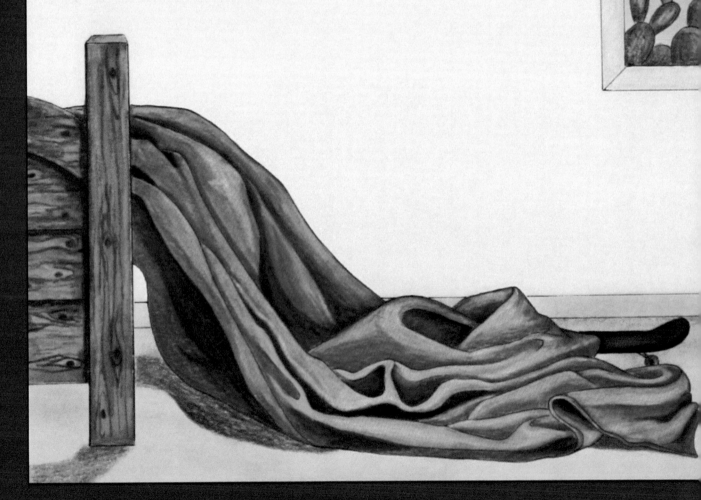

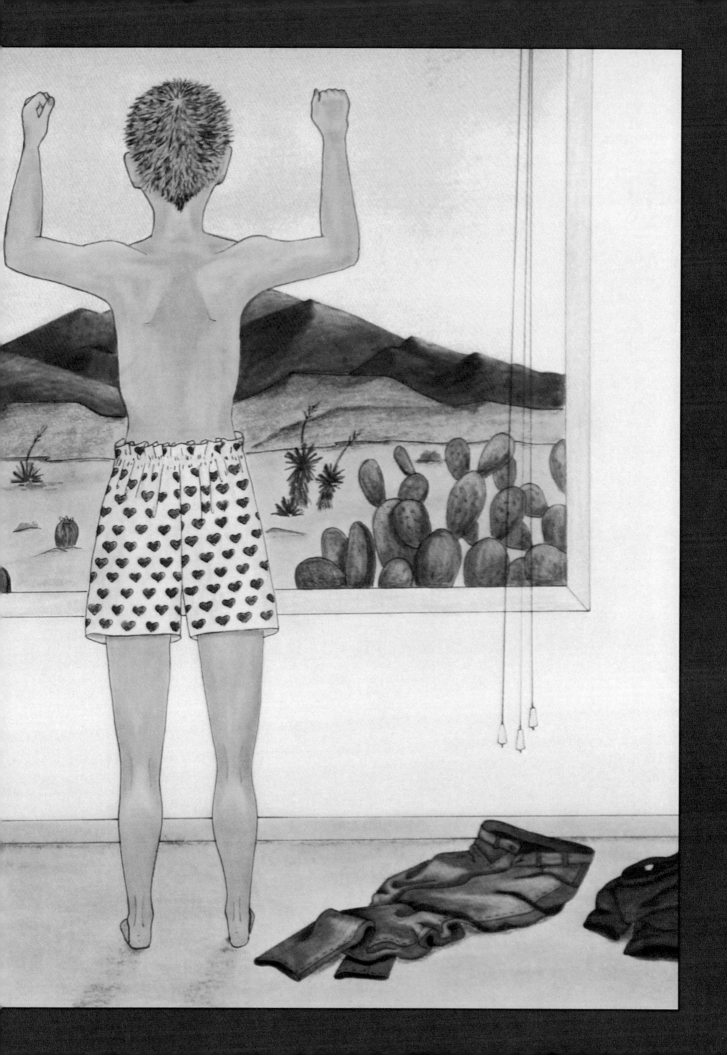

Jacob brushed his teeth, making silly faces in the mirror. He carefully picked out what to wear. After he got dressed, he met his father at the breakfast table.

"What is going on?" his father asked. "You got up today without me prying you out of bed."

Jacob laughed. "It's Valentine's Day, and I can't wait to get to school."

Now it was his father's turn to laugh. "Well, I never thought I would hear those words from you."

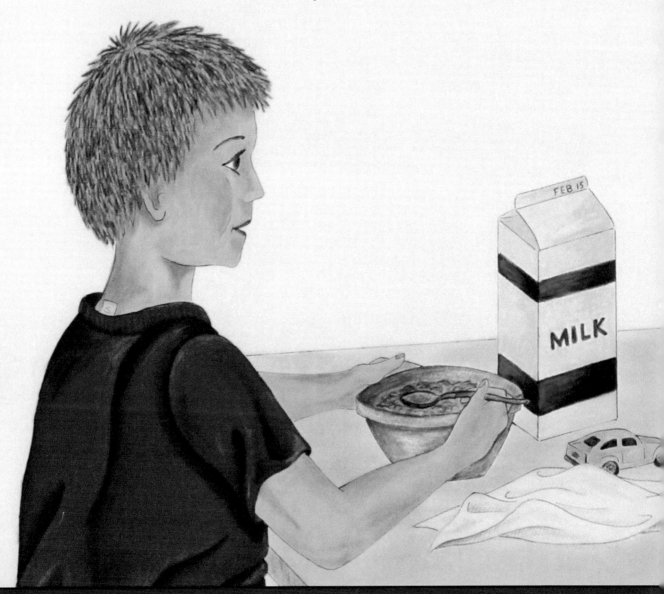

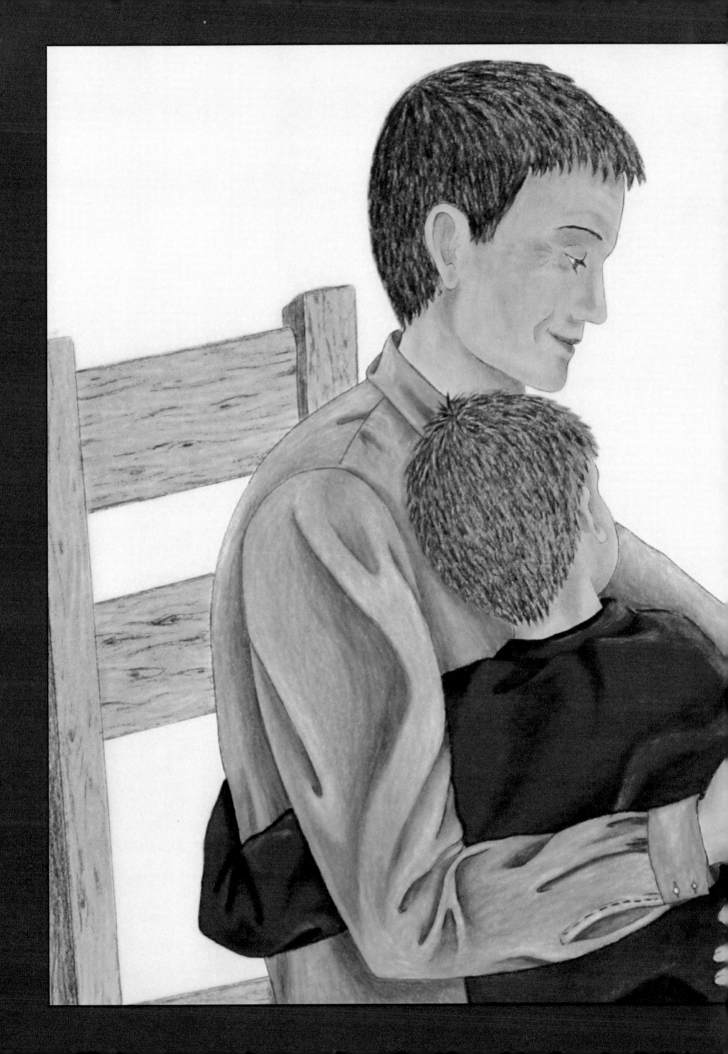

Jacob slurped down his cereal so fast he barely tasted it.
He grabbed his jacket and headed toward the door. Then he
remembered something and returned to the kitchen.

"Hey, Dad," he said as he gave his father a big hug.
"Happy Valentine's Day."

"Happy Valentine's Day to you, too." Jacob's father
returned the big hug.

Jacob hurried out the front door, hopped on his bike,
and sped off to school.

At school he fidgeted in his seat and impatiently watched the clock. His teacher, Mrs. Romero, had promised the class that at the end of the day, the students could share candy and make valentines.

Candy always excited Jacob. Today, however, the candy was just an afterthought. Jacob could not wait to make a special card for his mother.

The day dragged on. Math seemed to take forever. Reading lasted way too long. Even recess, Jacob's favorite time of day, didn't pass by fast enough.

Finally, it was two o'clock, and Mrs. Romero brought out the art supplies. Stacks of red, pink, and white construction paper were on the crafts table, along with a box containing silky ribbon, fuzzy yarn, and dainty strips of lace. The students lined up at the table to find the perfect materials for their special valentines.

A year ago this project would have made Jacob sad. But this year he was excited and couldn't wait to start.

When it was Jacob's turn to get supplies, he
picked bright-red paper. His mother had always
loved the color red. He also found some pieces
of fancy white lace that were just perfect.

He hurried back to his seat and got to work.
He cut out a large, beautiful heart and carefully
glued the lace around the edge.

On the heart he wrote, "I LOVE YOU
MOM" in big letters. He also wrote a special
note on a separate piece of paper. When he
finished, he asked Mrs. Romero to punch holes
in the heart and the note. This was part of his
well-thought-out plan.

Jacob sat in his seat and waited impatiently for the final bell to ring. His special valentine and special note were carefully tucked into his backpack.

Riiiing, sounded the bell. Jacob shot out of his seat and flew out the door. He left school so fast he completely forgot to say good-bye to Mrs. Romero or any of his friends.

Jacob did not take his usual route home. Instead he peddled his way to the gift shop. Inside the store, he scanned the shelves for chocolate candy. His mother loved chocolate. He found exactly what he wanted: a small chocolate heart wrapped in shiny, red foil.

Next, he went to the counter where balloons were sold. Jacob chose three balloons. The first shimmering, silver balloon had the words "I love you" written on it. "Happy Valentine's Day" was written on the second balloon, a bright-red one. The third glistening balloon read, "I miss you."

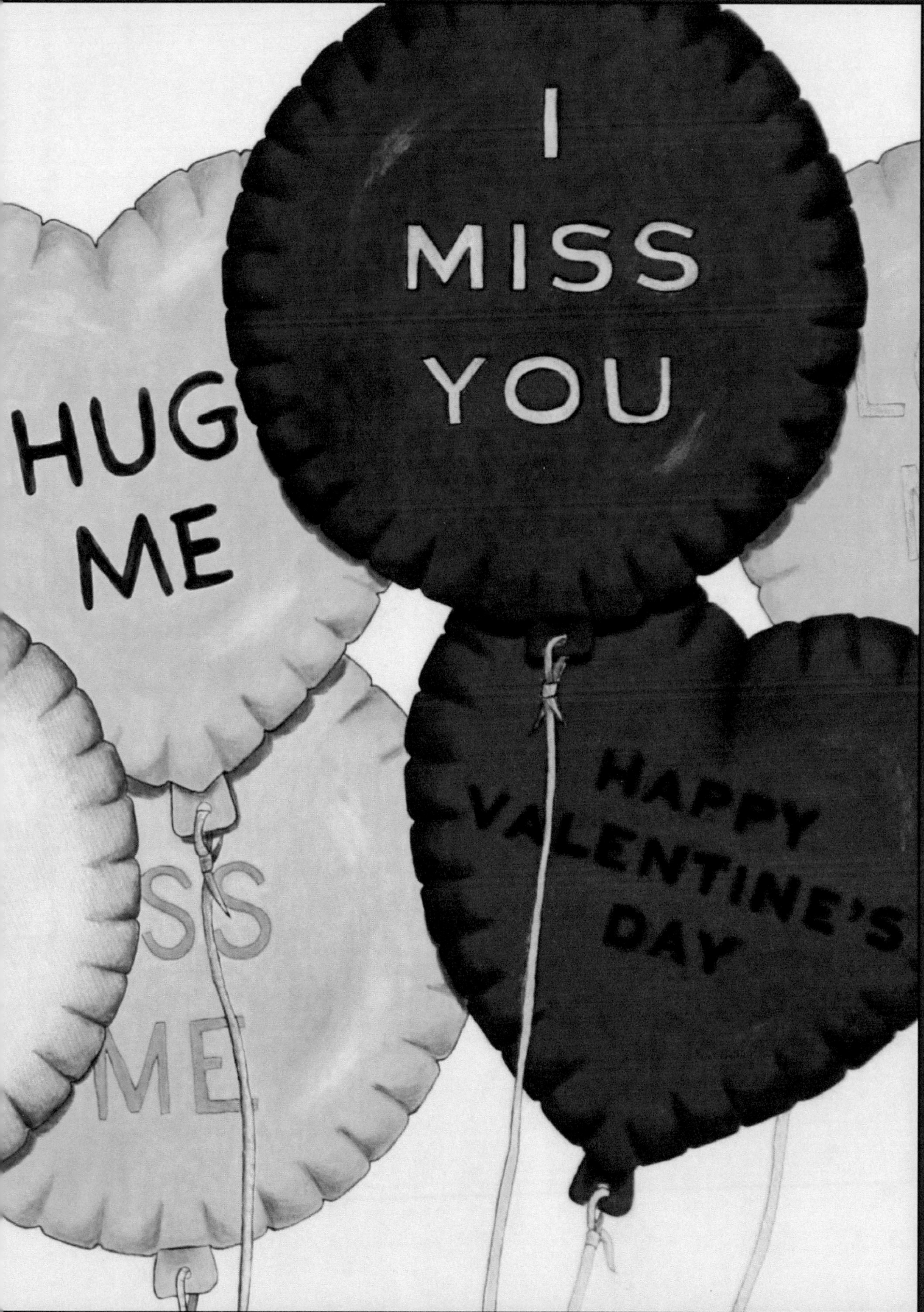
I MISS YOU
HUG ME
HAPPY VALENTINE'S DAY

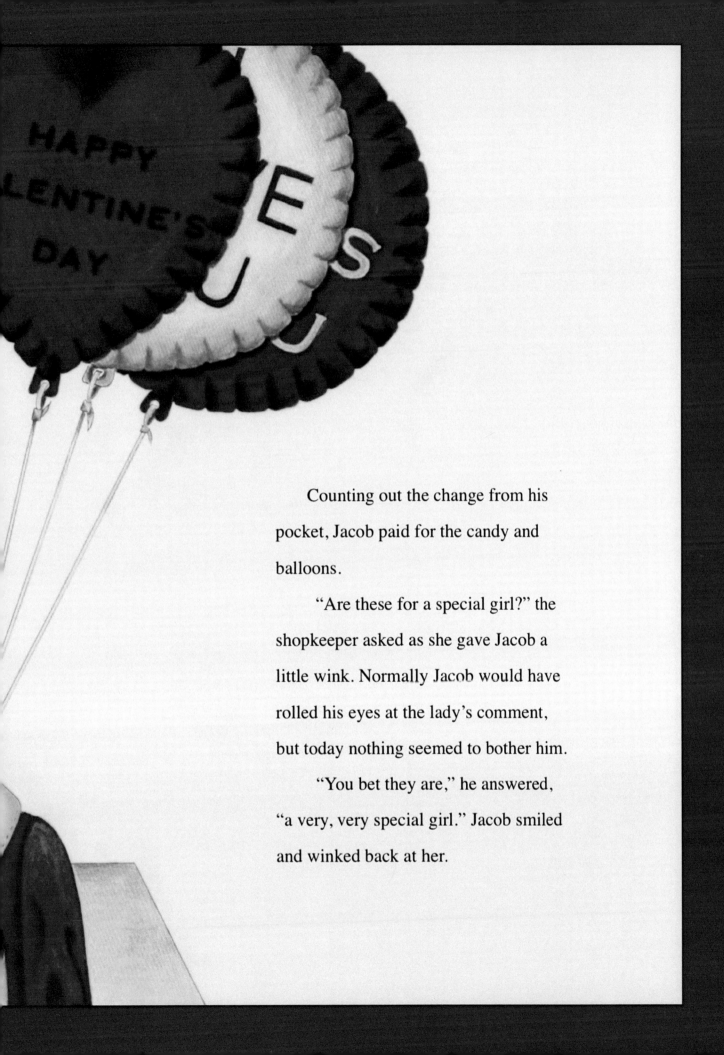

Counting out the change from his
pocket, Jacob paid for the candy and
balloons.

"Are these for a special girl?" the
shopkeeper asked as she gave Jacob a
little wink. Normally Jacob would have
rolled his eyes at the lady's comment,
but today nothing seemed to bother him.

"You bet they are," he answered,
"a very, very special girl." Jacob smiled
and winked back at her.

Back outside the store, Jacob tied the balloons to his bike. He sped off. The balloons bounced noisily behind the bike, sounding like popcorn popping.

Jacob laughed to himself, thinking, "I look like I am ready for the Fourth of July parade instead of Valentine's Day." And that he did. The red and silver balloons shimmered in the sunlight as he peddled his bike. He was wearing blue jeans, a blue baseball cap, and, in honor of Valentine's Day, his favorite red shirt.

He biked past the soccer field. He peddled past the park. He zoomed past his best friend's house. Ordinarily, Jacob might have stopped at these places, but not today. Today was special, and Jacob had to finish his important plan.

At the end of Cactus Street, Jacob got off his bike and leaned it against the wall next to a large, heavy gate. He untied the balloons from his bike and walked through the gate. It creaked a familiar creak as Jacob closed it behind him.

Once inside the gate, he carefully tied the strings of the three balloons together with a knot. The end of each string had a purpose. He took the tiny, brightly wrapped chocolate out of his pocket and tied the end of one of the strings around it. Jacob slipped the second string through the hole in the big paper heart and made a knot. He tied the final string to the special note he had written. His plan was almost complete.

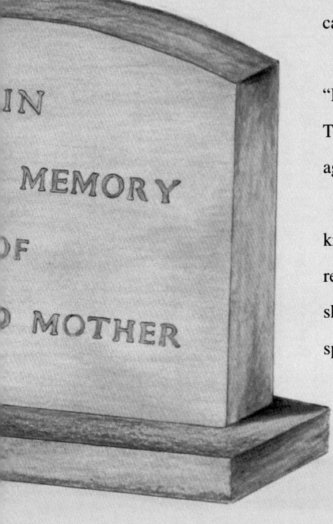

Jacob walked down a narrow path. He knew this path well. He cried every time he walked it. Today, tears were in his eyes, but for the first time, the tears came because he was so very, very happy. He walked until he came to a stone marker.

On the stone were written the words "In Loving Memory -Wife and Mother." The marker had been placed there two years ago, after Jacob's mother had died.

Jacob's heart pounded in his chest. He knelt down next to the gravestone. Before releasing the balloons, he looked up to the sky. He wiped away his tears and read the special note he had written.

"These valentines are for you, Mom.

I LOVE YOU

HAPPY VALENTINE'S DAY

I MISS YOU

Please catch my valentines in the sky."

Sending a Message

Death is part of life. It is hard to accept and understand. When our loved ones die, we miss them and wish we could be with them again. Although we cannot see them, we can send them messages.

These special messages help us say good-bye. They also allow us to tell our loved ones how we feel. On special days, such as Valentine's Day or birthdays, when we miss our loved ones the most, sending them messages helps us keep them alive in our memories.

PLEASE
Be Kind to Planet Earth

Sending a message to a loved one is a special event. This message is even sweeter if it is done in an eco-friendly way. Here are suggestions on ways to do this.

–Send a balloon message using 100-percent-biodegradable balloons. The message can be written directly on the balloon without using paper notes and strings. Only the biodegradable balloon is released.

–Write your message on a candle with marker or pen. As the candle burns, your message will disappear as it is sent to your loved one. Never use matches or light a candle without an adult present. Do not leave candles unattended.

–Collect a leaf from a tree. Write your message on the leaf. On a windy day, allow the wind to carry your message away.

–If you live by, or visit, the beach, write a message in the sand. The waves will carry your message to your loved one. Never go close to water without an adult.

–Blow bubbles. Before blowing bubbles, whisper your message. Your message will be carried away on the bubbles.

–Find a dandelion puffball. Whisper your message. As you blow away the puffball, your message will be carried with it.

–Write a special message to your loved one on the empty pages at the back of this book. You can read your message to your loved one again and again.

Special Messages

Special Messages

About the Author and Illustrator

JoAnne DeKeuster grew up near the small town of Waumandee, Wisconsin. She received a BA in art education from the University of Wisconsin–Eau Claire. Continuing her study of art at Northern Arizona University, she received a master's degree in ceramics. Jo worked as an art educator and gymnastics coach for over twenty years. She currently resides in Taos, New Mexico. She is an accomplished ceramic artist, and she and her husband operate Enchanted Circle Pottery.

46091002R00028

Made in the USA
San Bernardino, CA
26 February 2017